Turtle Sunrise

By Ann Higginbottom

Paintings by Lauren Spindle

ISBN 987-0-9791140-1-4

Written with love for Jed, Ellen and John-
I treasure our shared memories of sea turtles,
summer time and Amelia.

With immeasurable gratitude to Robby-
thank you for giving my words life and learning
to love the beach as much as I do.

ONCE UPON A TURTLE TIME,
Rising from the sea,
An island nestled off the coast
As happy as could be.

The beloved island teemed with life—
With families, friends and fish.
The beaches worn by love and time
Were every turtle's wish.

Every day Mom rode the waves
In search of her new nest.
The tiny island caught her eye;
She stopped and took a rest.

Every night the sun would set
As children climbed in bed.
But guided by the moon so bright,
Our Mom to shore would head.

Picking out a spot with care,
She dug a hole just right.
Her busy flippers tossed the sand—
Mom worked throughout the night.

The ocean crashed with songs of joy
As moonlight cast its glow.
Heaven was the audience
To this amazing show.

One by one, Mom laid us down
And placed us in cool sand.
Eighty-four in all, we were—
A family rather grand!

She gently covered us with sand
And tucked us all in place,
Then turned to face the ocean deep
And trusted in God's grace.

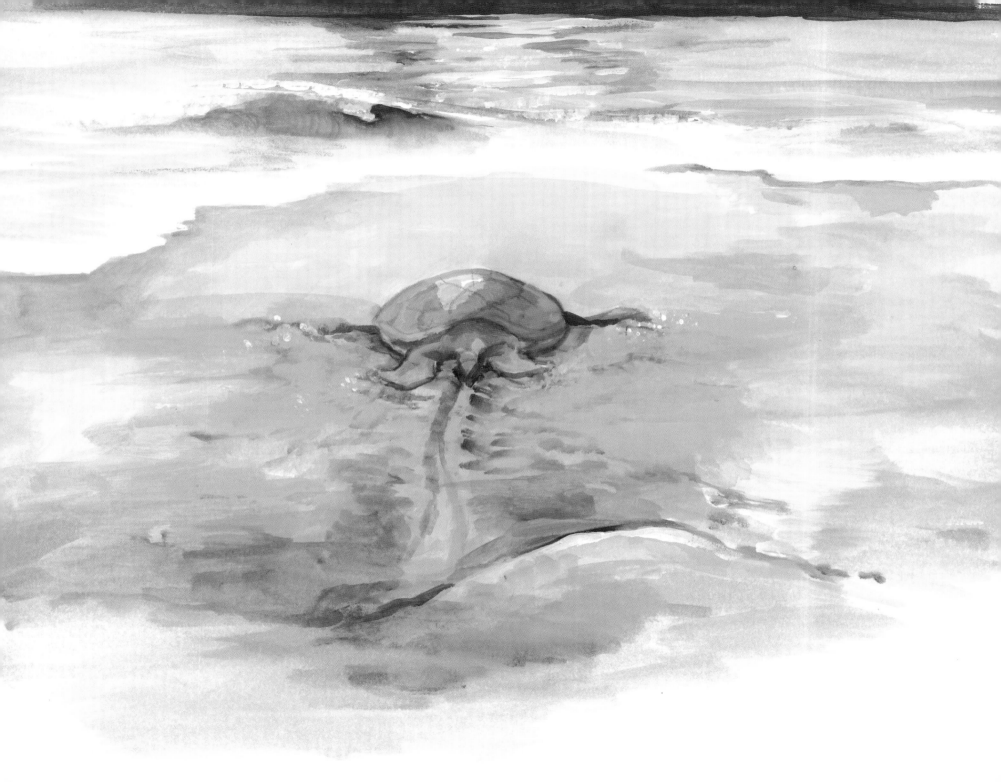

Two months went by, our eggs began
To grow with life and joy.
We waited in the silent nest,
Each turtle girl and boy.

One night the moon was ready, right,
And awe filled every shell.
God's gentle call we answered
With a wiggle and a swell.

We pecked and scurried all we could—
The hole was deep for flippers new!
Near the bottom of the nest,
Winkle, Pringle and Tom, too.

Above our heads, a scuttling sound—
Turtles moving towards the sea!
The moonlight led our siblings home—
All of them, but three.

The night gave way to sunrise—
We were stuck and running late.
Brothers, sisters all were gone,
But we just had to wait.

Two days passed and then a noise
Before the new day's light.
Above us, something moving now—
Sand and shells, then sight!

Loving hands then scooped us up,
Winkle, Pringle and Tom, too.
The Turtle Lady rescued us!
What joy! What hope! Woohoo!

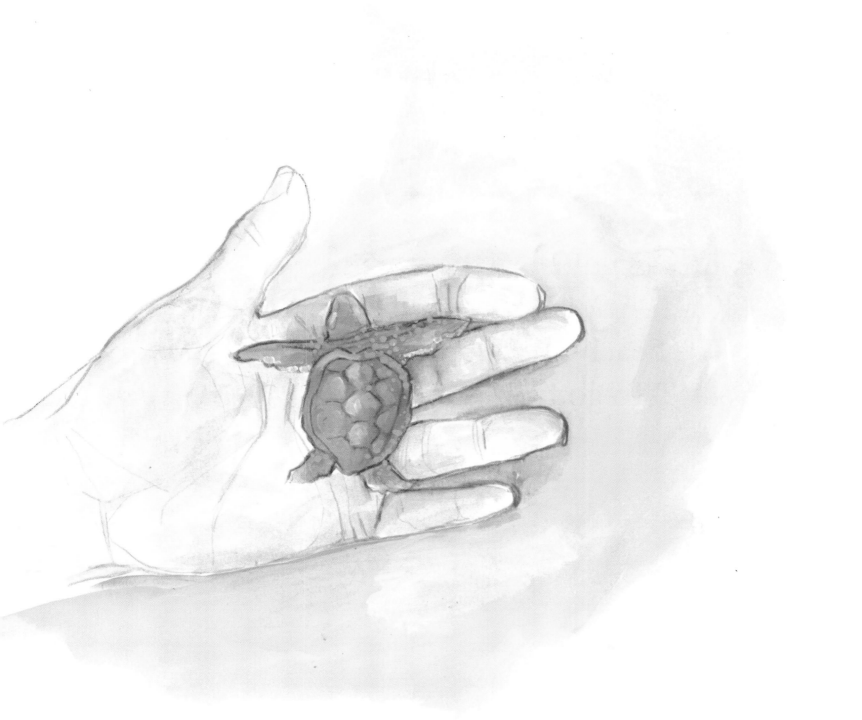

She placed us on the warming sand
And let us wiggle free.
The beach so big and we, so small,
To go from sand to sea!

The Turtle Lady took her time
And counted every shell.
She placed us in her bucket blue,
But why? We couldn't tell.

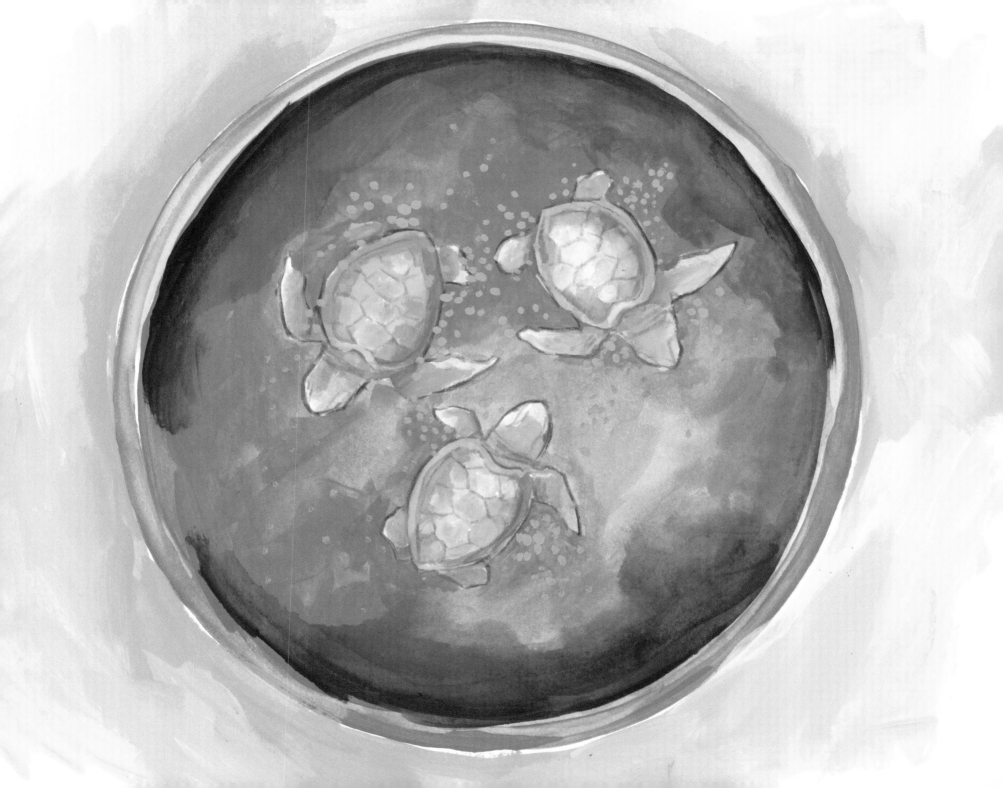

Moments passed and then the sky
Was moving up above.
The Turtle Lady took us
Towards the water that we love.

When first we saw the surf's great roar,
We cowered in our fright.
But then we thought with boldness:
"We must move with all our might!"

The Turtle Lady set us down
And showed us where to go.
With courage and with great delight
We chased the sunrise glow.

I am Winkle, first to go,
The leader from the start.
My flippers moved across the sand
With all my turtle heart.

Brother Pringle, right behind,
Stepped into my track.
He was doing rather well
And hardly looking back.

Tiny Tom was on the move
And putting up a fight.
His flipper sure was plenty strong,
But only on his right.

The Turtle Lady saw him
As he tottered up the beach,
But no matter how he wandered,
He was never out of reach.

She picked him up and turned him round
And helped him on his way.
Then Pringle and I called his name,
"Hurry, Tom! Let's play!"

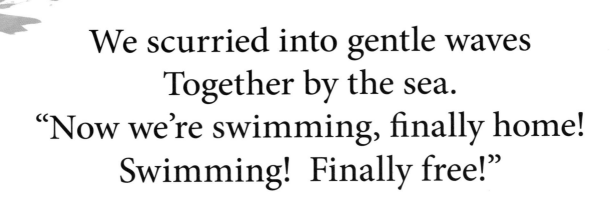

We scurried into gentle waves
Together by the sea.
"Now we're swimming, finally home!
Swimming! Finally free!"

The Turtle Lady watched with joy—
We saw our faithful friend.
But she had seen this all before,
And this was not the end.

The ocean grand before us
And our island small behind,
We hoped that we would come again
To shores and friends so kind.

We are big sea turtles now,
With stories left to tell.
Every year we come back here
To play and swim and dwell.

Little children, watch for us,
Winkle, Pringle and Tom, too.
We're part of God's creation,
Like the beach, the birds and you.